I HAVE A TALE TO TELL

Paul Theroux meets Anthony Bourdain. The interactions are personal and cover a lot of distance in these short stories giving readers a fresh look into the people, places, and cultures.

The book doesn't fit any genre. Short Story? Travel? Memoir? Essay? It goes beyond all these categories by distilling the essence of people and places in the author's short conversations with his Uber/Taxi drivers, while at the same time leading to some unexpected personal discoveries.

The bite-sized stories include a range of interactions - A Buddhist monk-in-training driving an Uber to make ends meet, but questioning the evils of materialism. A descendant of Genghis Khan (removed 20 generations) helping the author place "Kirgheestan" on the map. A former circus daredevil looking for infinite calm in Key West, and losing a few wives in the process. A Somalian transplant relying on her faith to drive in treacherous weather. And many more stories that scratch beneath the surface of the mundane and the ordinary.

THE UBER CHRONICLES

MINI STORIES ON THE GO

RAKESH GAMBHIR

This is a work of fiction. All of the characters, names, incidents, organizations, and dialogue in this novel are either the products of the author's imagination or are used fictitiously.

Archway Publishing books may be ordered through booksellers or by contacting:

Archway Publishing
1663 Liberty Drive
Bloomington, IN 47403
www.archwaypublishing.com
844-669-3957

ISBN: 978-1-6657-2428-9 (sc)
ISBN: 978-1-6657-2429-6 (e)

Library of Congress Control Number: 2022909570

Print information available on the last page.

Archway Publishing rev. date: 6/30/2022

CONTENTS

ACKNOWLEDGMENTS

I dedicate this short story collection to my kids, Nupur and Ratik, both incessant travelers and adventurers. Call it compromise or evolution, but I was forced to evaluate fresh perspectives and new ways of thinking, which ultimately led me to shed some redundant notions. I am thankful for that, but the journey is not complete yet. We will all continue growing together.

Special thanks to my wife Mona for being supportive of my literary efforts over the years.

TOURISTS DON'T KNOW WHERE THEY'VE BEEN,
TRAVELERS DON'T KNOW WHERE THEY'RE GOING.

—PAUL THEROUX

PROLOGUE

Each journey is unique. Even the mundane ones that take you from point A to point B or point X to point Y. Did you just get physically transported? Or did you also travel down this long corridor of time and space that was its own universe? In the process, you absorbed the sights and sounds of your journey, and reached your destination a little richer from the experience.

That's how I approached all my Uber trips when I traveled for business or personal reasons. And what a menagerie of people I met: housewives, students, ex-convicts, bootleggers, peddlers, hustlers, the "corporate suits," part-timers, the faithful, the rebels, the seekers, and the healers. All of them were playing their small side roles in this gig economy. And all of them had a tale to tell.

Maybe it was the close proximity or the closed spaces that took away inhibitions and made the drivers talk. Sometimes, the talk was mundane, but oftentimes, it was deep and personal. In a normal milieu, some of the questions I asked wouldn't have been welcome, but in that intimate setting, I always got an answer.

The short stories are a result of those small adventures. I hope you enjoy them as much as I enjoyed conversing with my drivers.

PEOPLE IN SLEEPING BAGS ARE THE SOFT TACOS OF THE BEAR WORLD.

—UNKNOWN

THE BEAR WHISPERER

"Where are you from?"

"Colorado."

"What are you doing in Texas?"

"Jobs, jobs, and jobs." Jared continued, "To be honest with you, I am completely lost. I had a good forest ranger job out there. But the forest service decided to cut payroll, so here I am. I'm living in my sister's basement and just survive on whatever work I can get."

"That's got to be rough," I said sympathetically. "But don't you miss the Rockies?"

"Definitely. The mountains were my lifeline." Jared pointed to a cutout, hanging from the rearview mirror. I looked closely at it and saw a mountain range enveloped by blue skies.

"I spent some time in Denver," I said. "Tried a few hikes, but I couldn't handle being alone in all that wilderness. I was very worried about the bears."

"Bears?" His weathered face broke into a smile. "They are gentle souls."

"Gentle?" I repeated.

"Depends upon the situation." Jared paused, looking over his shoulder into the blind spot. "You can either run or play dead when you spot a bear."

"I see."

"But first, you must shout out 'Hello bear!' in a loud voice." The car gently changed lanes. "The bear might just ignore you and walk away."

"And if he doesn't walk away?"

"Well, if the bear seems to be in a good mood, you crumple up in the fetal position and play dead. If he appears in a foul mood, you just cut and run."

"And how will I know if the bear is feeling like a Boy Scout or a serial killer?"

We stopped at a red light. He seemed to be relishing the role of a wildlife expert, mixing in facts on animal psychology.

"You gotta go with your heart." Jared looked back at me. "It's a split-second decision."

We were moving again.

"Huh. You are telling me that I greet the bear, and if he doesn't reciprocate, I listen to my heart."

"Sometimes you gotta take a chance." He shrugged philosophically.

"Okay," I mumbled.

"So these rules apply to all bears?" I asked. "Male or female; young or old; black or brown; regular or grizzly?"

"Not at all," Jared replied. "They all react differently. They are like people, all with different personalities."

"Then there are no set rules in a bear encounter?" I asked, a little conflicted.

"Well, it's a roll of the dice." Jared chuckled. "Just like a blind date."

Sure, my man. A blind date could turn into a long, blissful marriage or a gruesome murder.

"But don't overthink this." He slowed down a little behind another car. "You have more time than you think and more choices than you realize."

Comforting words coming from the Bear Whisperer (and the only thing Jared whispered was the clichés).

As we rolled along to our destination, I was thinking about the conflicting advice. Sure, my Uber driver turned life coach. I must listen to my heart when a bear sizes me up as a snack with his morning latte.

"Makes sense," was all I could squeak out, though.

Jared followed the warp of the road, to turn right for the drop-off point that was coming up shortly.

"Thanks for the bear tips," I said, getting out.

"Enjoy your hike next time you are in Colorado." Jared waved goodbye. "The bears are mostly in a good mood. And if you meet them," he called out the open window, "try savoring the moment. Don't rush it."

Author's Notes: There is a lot of conflicting literature on bear encounters and how humans should best approach one. There is no clear consensus, and as our man Jared pointed out, it's a roll of the dice.

The book *A Walk in the Woods* by Bill Bryson chronicles the author's undertaking to walk the Appalachian Trail. Bill is also deathly afraid of bears. And there is a chapter dedicated to his research on bear attacks and how to avoid them. His conclusions are the same as mine. There is no clearly established rhyme and reason for bear attacks. The fact of the matter is, no one can tell you what to do in case of a bear attack.

I DON'T KNOW THE REASON.
STAYED HERE ALL SEASON.
WITH NOTHING TO SHOW BUT THAT BRAND NEW TATTOO.
HELL YES, IT HURTS,
BUT IT'S A REAL BEAUTY

—JIMMY BUFFET, "MARGARITAVILLE"

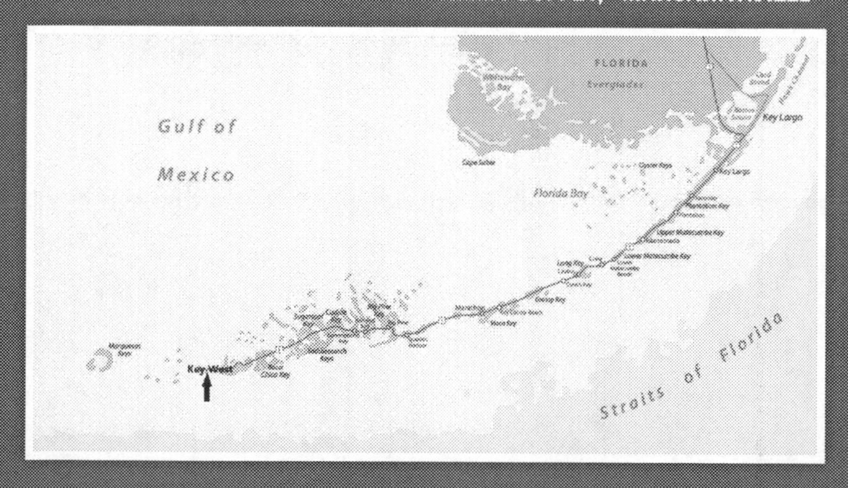

KEY WEST—EVERYTHING IS NORTH OF HERE

It was the wee hours of the morning.

"Anybody care for the key lime special, before we call it a day?" the bartender called out. "On the house."

"Key lime pie," I chirped. "That sounds great."

"No. Just rum that recently arrived from Cuba."

Laughter filled the room. Little did we know that the bartender was using local code to refer to smuggled Cuban rum. Me and my wife, along with our lifelong friends, the Koppels, had just driven from Miami. Following the smell of the ocean, we meandered our way to this dive bar by the water.

"How will we get to the hotel this late, after all this?" I croaked.

"Ever heard of Uber?"

There was more laughter.

Within an hour, all four of us were seated in the back of a Honda and being driven, very slowly, to the local Marriott, through the jagged strip that is Key West. "Margaritaville" softly played in the background.

"Where are you guys from?" Houdini asked.

"Ohio."

"Where's that?"

It was an obvious joke on the ignominious nature of the state of Ohio.

"Somewhere north of here," I said, trying to be funny.

"Everything is north of here," Houdini drawled gently, drawing attention to the fact that Key West is the southernmost city in the mainland United States.

Houdini, our driver, was a gentle-looking man with a long, proud beard, almost as if he had lost his scissors and trimmers years back. The flat hat he wore completed the vintage look. But what stood out most was his soft, sad eyes that told of unspoken pains in the past. Houdini had been an escape artist at a traveling circus, in his past life, where no stunt was off-limits.

He was born Frankie to an Italian family, but at the circus, they called him the Magician and named him "the new-age Houdini." Then one day, the magic didn't materialize. The mishap left Houdini with two broken legs and large unpaid bills. After a long rehab, he sought out a quieter and more peaceful life for himself in Key West, and was now driving us back to the hotel.

"Why not move to a bigger city like Miami?" I asked, pointing out the employment options available in a big city.

"In Miami, time flies. In Key West, it stops," he calmly replied.

"How does that work?"

"You have to live here to figure that out."

"This place is, what, five miles long? Too small."

"That's the whole point."

"But what are you looking for?"

"Peace and quiet."

"For how long?"

"Forever."

I opened the windows, and a cool ocean breeze

drifted in. We were silent for a while as the car rolled down the empty street.

"I came with my wife to Key West for a few weeks," Houdini finally said. "We never went back."

That, I later learned, pretty much summed up the mindset of all the transplants from the mainland United States, who came to Key West and never went back.

"I think we should stay in Key West one more day," I said.

"Let's go back to Miami," Mona, my wife, said. "More shopping."

Soon, it was guys vs. gals, in a heated battle about tomorrow's plans.

"Guys, you should listen to your wives," Houdini softly interjected. "I have been married three times, so I should know."

We all looked at each other and laughed at the irony of it.

"Maybe you didn't listen enough," Mona said. "And the first two drifted away."

"Drifted away is correct, lady," Houdini spoke in a defeated tone. "The first one went in the hurricane of 1992."

"Oh, we are so sorry," we all said together, in shock.

"No, it's okay," Houdini continued, talking as he turned left toward the hotel. "I wouldn't leave the island when the hurricanes came, despite the warnings. But my wife left for the shelters in Miami and never came back."

"And the second one?"

"Well, she left for a shopping trip to Miami, and guess what happened?" Houdini looked at us in the rearview mirror. "I think they all loved me, but living in Key West year-round, being as small and narrow as it is, can be difficult."

All was quiet in the car for a while as we pondered this.

"So once they go to Miami," Mona said, picking up the thread that led to disappearing wives, "they don't want to come back."

"Seems like."

After another stretch of silence, Houdini broke it by saying, "I think I love my third wife more than ever. But she's been clamoring for a girls' weekend out to Miami lately."

We all laughed, even more, wondering if it was an elaborate joke or indeed a typical Key West happening.

Author's Notes: Key West, a narrow strip of land, is the southernmost point in the mainland United States. Just ninety miles from Cuba, Key West is famous for its imported, and sometimes smuggled, rum. The iconic, relaxed way of life in Key West draws people from all over the United States, and some of them just stay forever. But some people may find it too small and restrictive.

Ernest Hemingway spent his last years in Key West. Jimmy Buffet was so inspired by it that he wrote the song "Margaritaville." The song conjures up visions of a place where time stands still, and a man can forever nurse a frozen concoction of tequila, lime, and a little salt, in front of a setting sun by the ocean.

THE THINGS YOU OWN END UP OWNING YOU. IT'S ONLY AFTER YOU LOSE EVERYTHING THAT YOU'RE FREE TO DO ANYTHING.

— CHUCK PALAHNIUK, *FIGHT CLUB*

3

SPIRITS IN A MATERIAL WORLD

Here he is. My Uber driver in crimson robes, sporting horn-rimmed glasses and a clean-shaven head, just like the Dalai Lama. Dorze was smiling, ever so peacefully, as the mad Houston traffic whizzed by.

"Going to a costume party?"

Dorze threw his head back and laughed uproariously. "I am training to be a Buddhist monk." His chuckles finally settled down. "Working through my final vows. But gotta pay the bills man."

"You have a Texan drawl?" I asked.

"I was born here, but my parents are practicing Buddhists from Tibet," Dorze clarified. "I asked a lot of questions about God when I was young."

"That's normal," I said. "Every kid is curious."

"I shouldn't have been." He sighed. "My parents dispatched me to a monastery in Tibet to answer my questions and become a monk."

"Bye-bye childhood," I laughed dryly.

"Such a bummer!" Dorze looked at me reflectively.

"How was your experience at the monastery?" I was curious.

"It was nonstop suffering, penitence, and chastity." He rolled his eyes.

It was my turn to laugh.

Dorze turned serious. "But I learned a few things about the human condition."

"So why not join the material world?" I said. "What's in it for you now?"

"Well, this is all I know now." Dorze abruptly changed lanes with minimal inspection of his rearview mirror. "And you know what? There is immense suffering in this world. I think humanity needs all the help it can get."

"Why is there suffering in this world?"

"Because of the desire." He fell into a thoughtful silence. "We want and crave more of everything. More love. More power. More money. More emotion. More attachments."

"Isn't that the whole point of living?" I said, somewhat agitated. "What's wrong with it?"

"More will not fill our soul."

"So, what's the answer?"

"Stop craving. Stop wanting."

"You mean the human race should stop dreaming?" Maybe I was taking Dorze too literally.

Dorze braked hard into the upcoming bend in the road and accelerated up the freeway. The momentary jolt pushed me against the seat. And in the throes of brief panic, I thought this guy might be a spiritual master, but he needed a little more finesse in the laws of the physical world.

"The human race needs a spiritual rebirth," Dorze said, weaving in and out of lanes at will on the expressway.

Great words of wisdom to live up to—if this driving didn't kill us first.

"Desire is the engine of humanity," I continued a little plaintively. "What would a man be without love, attachments, hunger for greatness?" I looked outside the window and noticed the airport signs coming up. "Not wanting, not desiring—that can't be the answer!"

"Well, letting go is the only answer Buddha found two thousand years back." He forced his foot down on the accelerator and quickly cut through the traffic, only to slow down when our car got too close to the winking brake lights of the car ahead.

"What's the answer then, two thousand years later?"

Dorze let out a deep, low breath. "Keep suffering."

"How about finding a balance between the spiritual and the material world?"

"That's like applying a Band-Aid to a knife wound." Dorze abruptly changed lanes again. "You can't put the toothpaste back into the tube."

"Toothpaste?" I asked. "What does that have to do with suffering?"

"The human race has caged itself in the vicious cycle of desire and possession." His hands left the wheel and pantomimed squeezing toothpaste out of a tube. "There is no going back."

Please get your hands back on the steering, I thought to myself.

"I thought humanity was about hope and redemption."

He fell quiet, then finally spoke as if in a trance. "We need to stop conquering time and space and instead feed our souls." I saw him almost close his eyes. "Then the universe will be saved."

"What does that mean?"

"I am not sure, man," he said weakly. "I am confused too."

"I am glad we sorted that out." I laughed. "Good timing. We are here ten minutes early, thanks to your speedy driving."

I got out of the car and entered the material world.

Author's Notes: Gurus have been looking for the "answer" for thousands of years. Not surprisingly, Dorze was confused. But searching for the answer itself is a good start. Taking an inventory of our baggage (physical and mental) and reducing the footprint of desire might be a positive undertaking.

WHY DID GOD MAKE WOMEN SO BEAUTIFUL
AND MAN WITH SUCH A LOVING HEART?

— WALKER PERCY, *LOVE IN THE RUINS*

COULD THIS BE LOVE?

"What's this chocolate chip cookie smell?"

"I bake cookies in a bakery," Edmundo replied. "Driving is my part-time gig."

"What are your hours?"

"I normally drive in the late afternoon hours from two to five," he said, "and head over to my girlfriend's house after. Play with my baby boy, cook with my girlfriend, and spend some time together." He smiled. "I am a lucky guy."

"That sounds cool," I said encouragingly. "And back to work tomorrow, huh?"

"Nah, my wife wanted me to take her to the mall tomorrow." Edmundo looked around before making the turn. "She hardly takes a day off."

"You mean your girlfriend."

"No, my wife."

Silence while I tried to sort this through.

The rain had just subsided, but Edmundo drove with certainty on the wet roads. He was a short and slender guy, dark-skinned, and possessed a signature laugh that hung in the air a little bit after it had finished. And smelled of chocolate chip cookies. That itself is enough to drive women crazy for this guy.

"Does your wife know about your girlfriend?"

"No way. She will be devastated. Can't do that."

"Does your girlfriend know about your wife?"

"No, man. I can't hurt her feelings. She is the mother of my child."

"I see," I said, a little half-seriously. "You don't want to hurt either of the two—your wife and girlfriend."

"Me and my wife, we used to live in the same neighborhood. We went to the same church. Dated briefly. Then she came to America while I stayed back, doing my thing. And when mayhem broke in Venezuela, we were all desperate. The government broke down, cartels all around. I was not making any money. Going hungry for days.

"You know what happened in Venezuela, right? My family went through stuff you can't imagine. Then, somehow, we got in touch, and she got me here. My wife works long hours at the hospital to support us. Very patient, very noble. I will always be grateful to her," Edmundo said. "She saved my life.

Wife

"And Jamie, when I first saw her, it's like I heard a new melody. When I finish driving and go to her apartment, it's like therapy, man. That pretty thing sits cross-legged across from me with our baby in her arms and listens to all the stuff I have to say. We walk to the park, and we swoop like birds floating on hot air. And we walk back holding hands, not saying a word, occasionally looking into each other's eyes. It's magical, man. It's an insanely beautiful feeling." Edmundo paused, almost choked up with emotion. "When we are sitting on the sofa, and I am running my fingers through her tangled hair," he couldn't stop talking, "she tells me I saved her."

"Nice!" I said with some gravity. "Your wife saved you, and you went ahead and saved this girl."

Edmundo was quiet as we took the last exit toward the airport.

Girlfriend

Okay, I get it. The girlfriend had a name, and the wife didn't. The girlfriend was Kim Kardashian and Julia Roberts rolled into one neat package, and the wife was Mother Teresa. And it was all matter-of-fact when talking about the wife, but poetry sprang forth from Edmundo when Jamie came up in discussion.

"You have put yourself in a tough situation," I finally said.

"What situation?"

"You are risking your future," I explained.

"It's a calculated risk."

"You are bending reality."

"Reality is that I am in love with both of them. And they both tell me that I smell like a biscuit."

"Aren't you deceiving both of them?"

Edmundo looked at me in the rearview mirror, and I thought he almost sneered at me. "This is the way love works, man."

There was a long line of cars as we approached the terminal.

"Drop me at the next gate," I told him. Getting out of the vehicle, I smiled and said, "All right, best of luck with both the women you love equally."

Edmundo flashed his teeth and drove off.

Author's Notes: Of all the Uber tales, this is the one where I felt a little conflicted. This was a man who was looking at life through a lens that very conveniently bent reality. Or maybe he was just conveniently delusional and played the part very convincingly.

There was nothing profound in what he said, but I couldn't question his love for both women—one love born out of gratitude and the other of pure passion. Edmundo had a very uncomplicated view of what love was and its many variations. He was grateful to his wife for rescuing him, but that didn't stop him from loving another woman. There was no deceit here. At least, in Edmundo's head. He didn't see a problem.

YOU WANT A FRIEND IN WASHINGTON? GET A DOG.

—HARRY S TRUMAN

MY DOG IS RUNNING FOR OFFICE

I entered the taxi through the rear door.

"That was some dogfight!" I heard a growl from the front seat. "Was that you growling?" I asked the driver.

"Not me," the driver said. "Meet my dog." He looked back. "He is all worked up about the first presidential debate."

Brewski, a small black dog with curious brown eyes, popped his head up, chewing on a bone.

"Yes," I replied. "This debate was nasty, man."

"I could do a better job in the debate." Brewski dug deeper into the bone.

"It's a dog-eat-dog world in Washington," I replied. "You think you can run with the big dogs?"

"Are you making fun of my small stature?" Brewski growled.

"You are taking me too literally, my friend," I said.

"It's not the size of the dog in the fight; it's the size

of the fight in the dog." Brewski took a savage bite of the bone.

"I will drain the swamp." Brewski was chewing on a sneaker now.

"Those politicians, they are all the same." I continued, "You can't teach old dogs new tricks."

"I will throw them a bone." Brewski had his face inside the shoe now. "Everybody can be leashed." Brewski started sniffing around.

"Brewski has to do his business." The driver stopped the car on the side of the freeway.

"And the economy? What are you going to do about it?"

"I will print money and give it to everyone in America."

"Isn't that what the government just did?"

"But they gave it all to the rich." Brewski sniffed around the bushes. "The not-so-rich are still working like dogs. It's the poor's turn to get something," Brewski said, getting in position to relieve himself on the grass.

"Every dog has his day," I mused.

"And COVID?" I inquired. "What will you do?"

"I have done the math," Brewski replied quickly. "Things will get better in the dog days of summer."

"Played any golf lately?" I asked, changing the subject.

"Yeah, I went." Brewski sighed. "But it was raining cats and dogs."

"What about race?"

"It's a sensitive issue."

"Now you are acting like a politician. Do you have a plan to fix this doggone issue?"

"Let me get back to you on this," Brewski said after a calculated pause.

"Who's your primary opponent?" I asked.

"You know, that guy."

"Who?"

"His bark is worse than his bite."

"If you lose?"

"I will keep fighting for this country." Brewski was eyeing a small wooden stick on the ground. "A cat has nine lives."

"But you are a dog."

"You are taking me too literally, my friend." Brewski took a deep breath and attacked the stick, shredding it to pieces.

Author's Notes: I never encountered a dog in an Uber ride. My son had recently adopted the dog when the first presidential debate happened. The acrimony and the lack of civility in the first debate brought forth the idea of using the dog as a medium to convey the message of civility and good manners—and point out the fact that politics is fraught with peril, and hyperbole is the name of the game.

"I AM" IS REPORTEDLY THE SHORTEST SENTENCE IN THE ENGLISH LANGUAGE. COULD IT BE THAT "I DO" IS THE LONGEST SENTENCE?

—GEORGE CARLIN

COULD THIS BE LOVE (PART DEUX)?

"What brings you out of the house, Grandpa?" I said, "You could be rocking in your armchair reading your newspaper." I quickly reminded him that "Grandpa" was a joke, and I was not a young person myself.

"Boredom. Making a little money," Pops replied. "But primarily the wife. Every time she has an errand for me, I go out and do a few rides. Get back home in the evening with the goods."

"She would forget what she asked for by the time you get home," I joked.

"She doesn't forget." Pops laughed. "Let me tell you a story."

> Once upon a time, an old couple lived together. As so happens with being

together for so long, things fell into a predictable routine. No big conflicts. Minor skirmishes on how to keep the gears of daily life moving, but peaceful in general.

One day, as the heavy snow covered the ground and the wind whistled around the frozen landscape, the wife started feeling cold. The wife wanted some more firewood.

"But there is firewood in the house," the old man protested.

"We might run out," the wife replied. "And then we will freeze."

The man knew enough not to protest. He picked up his ax, braced himself for the bitter cold, and silently walked out in the white fog that shrouded the landscape.

He walked along the edge of the forest, circled back to the frozen lake, and aimlessly wandered a little more. He came upon the local tavern. The fire crackled with warmth, and the place was aglow with the laughter of friends. And as we know, time flies.

By the time he got home, it was dark. The fire was out, and the old lady was sitting, all wrapped up in blankets.

"I missed you," the old man said with a feeling that hadn't surfaced for many years.

"Did you get the firewood?" the old lady asked without missing a beat.

I laughed.

I also noticed he had taken a long way home. Fine by me. The "Once Upon a Time" story was totally worth it for its lack of a happy ending.

"What do you say to your wife, then, once you reach home?"

"I tell her I love her."

Sweet. "And your wife, what does she say?"

"Did you get the milk?"

The car cut across the highway, traveled a couple of blocks, and stopped in front of my house.

"So, what's on the shopping list tonight?" I asked innocently.

"More milk."

"She loves you," I said, getting out of the car.

"Yes, that's likely true." The driver shrugged, driving off.

IT FEELS GOOD TO BE LOST IN THE RIGHT DIRECTION.

—UNKNOWN

WHERE IN THE WORLD IS KYRGYZSTAN?

"I could mistake you for Genghis Khan."

"Well, my friend," Genghis Jr. chuckled, "there is some truth to what you say. My family is directly descended from Genghis Khan."

"Is that so? How do you know that?" I asked out of curiosity.

"We have a long oral history, which says the great Khan conquered our lands and, as was customary with him, sired hundreds of children." Genghis Jr. explained further, "That started a few dynasties in the area. Fast forward eight hundred years and here I am."

"Siring kids and starting dynasties." I smiled. "That was probably his favorite hobby. What was it like growing up a Khan descendant?"

"Bedtime stories of Khan's exploits were told and

retold on a nightly basis," Genghis Jr. replied. "And we are all told to practice the Khan code."

"What's the Khan code?"

"Man's highest joy is in victory: to conquer one's enemies; to pursue them; to deprive them of their possessions; to make their beloved weep; to ride on their horses; and to embrace their wives and daughters," he blurted out robotically.

Oops! This was not the icebreaker I had in mind.

"Where are you from?"

"Kirgeestaahn."

"Kir-gee-staahn, huh?" I intoned slowly, trying to

emphasize the "gee." "I have heard about Pakistan and Afghanistan but not Kirgeestaahn. Where is this?"

"Central Asia."

"Close to the Middle East?" I asked casually.

"Not really." After a brief pause, Genghis Jr. said helpfully, "It's on the border with China."

"China is a large country with a large border, man." I let out a small laugh. "Which border would that be?"

"The central Asian border."

That was not telling me much.

"What's the nearest country?"

"Tajikistan."

That didn't ring any bells. I dug deep into my consciousness and desperately, almost frantically, searched for any memory of these two names.

Nothing. Nada. My mind was a blank slate.

Of course, it's not like there was ever any regular breaking news from Tajikistan on CNN. Nor were the weathermen weighing in on the tornadoes that touched down in Kirgeestaahn.

The situation was getting serious.

"What are the other countries nearby?" I asked cautiously, trying to get some handle on the situation.

"Turkmenistan and Uzbekistan."

I looked around the small Toyota Prius. There was a

tiny clang from the trunk as the car took a quick right turn. *Cleaning supplies*, I thought to myself.

"You keep this thing clean," I said, changing the subject.

But my mind was not clean. My own ignorance troubled some corner of my mind. All these years of watching Anthony Bourdain and it had come to this? I couldn't identify a good swath of Central Asia! Or perhaps the driver was just a sinister guy making up imaginary country names and playing with his helpless passengers.

We hit the sharp white fluorescent lighting of the approaching airport. Then it hit me. I took one final shot. "How far is Kazakhstan from Kirgeestaahn?" I said, getting out.

"That is one of the borders. At least you know something, my friend," Genghis Jr. laughed as he drove away.

Redemption.

Author's Notes: Later, some research disclosed the country we talked about is Kyrgyzstan (Kirgeestaahn).

There is a section of Central Asia that is relatively obscure to most people, primarily because these countries were originally part of the Soviet Republic but now are independent. These countries encompass large swaths of land. For example, Kazakhstan is the tenth largest country in the world by landmass.

The Genghis reference reflects the fact that Genghis Khan conquered many lands and, as spoils of victory, sired hundreds of children with the vanquished population. It is estimated there are sixteen million men alive today with his DNA.

Bruce: WHAT IF I NEED YOU? WHAT IF I HAVE QUESTIONS?
God: THAT'S YOUR PROBLEM, BRUCE. THAT'S EVERYBODY'S PROBLEM. YOU KEEP LOOKING UP.

—FROM THE MOVIE *BRUCE ALMIGHTY* STARRING MORGAN FREEMAN AS GOD AND JIM CARREY AS BRUCE

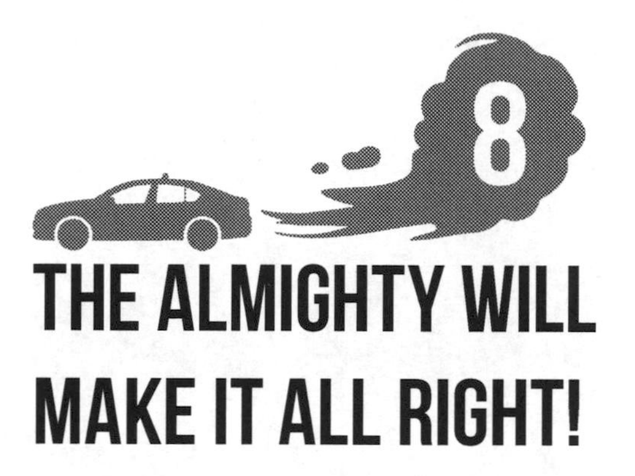

THE ALMIGHTY WILL MAKE IT ALL RIGHT!

The car veered off the icy road and continued sliding. As the vehicle approached the guardrail, the young lady at the wheel calmly steered the car back to the road. The event took all of two seconds while I braced for an impact. It was *not* a near-death experience, and no, my whole life didn't flash before my eyes in that instant. But my grip on the pizza box tightened. There were still two slices left, and I was not letting them go.

Impressive recovery, I thought, but kept my mouth shut.

It was late in the evening. The ice on the road sparkled like confetti on the brightly lit freeway. The patchy fog covered the skies with a blanket of gray and added another element of risk to the treacherous roads. The Uber driver ignored all the warning signs and snaked her way down Route 315, weaving in and out of lanes at will, occasionally ignoring a few laws of physics. You can also picture me sitting in the back seat, holding a large pizza box with both hands. Considering the driving, that was quite a balancing act.

Two minutes down the line, the skid happened again. The car veered, the driver waited calmly, and, at the last instant, took control of the vehicle.

"Can't you just focus on the driving?" I squeaked, trying not to sound fearful.

"It's nothing," the driver said casually. "That's how we drive in Minnesota. I just moved to Ohio. Driving in Ohio is a piece of cake."

That softened me up a little. Maybe this young girl knew something about driving on ice.

"What's your name?"

"Sirocco." She replied. "My parents named me after the hot strong winds that blow out of the Sahara desert"

With her driving, she sure is living up to her name, I thought to myself.

"And what country that would be?" I asked.

"Somalia."

I woke up.

"How long were you in Minnesota, Sirocco?"

"Three months."

"There are no icy roads in Somalia," I blurted out, quickly realizing Sirocco got her driving permit not long ago. And her teenage confidence bordered on delusional.

"No icy roads." Sirocco laughed. "And very few cars. I learned how to drive in Minnesota only. My grandpa taught me all the ropes, and he said to be calm when driving."

"Which you are," I said approvingly. "What else did your grandpa teach you?"

"He said to trust in the Almighty when the car starts sliding on ice."

"Trust in the Almighty?" I couldn't help stupidly repeating after her.

"The Almighty will make things right," young Sahra proclaimed with conviction. "Everything will take care of itself."

"I see," I said quietly. "So, the Almighty will correct the slide."

"Only if you believe in the Almighty," she replied strongly, speeding up a little.

I had no answer to that kind of reasoning.

Abandoning my grip on the pizza box, I silently hung on to the edge of the seat. Call it resignation, or a lack of control, but I was calm. What're a few more icy skids when the Almighty is going to make things all right?

Author's Notes: It takes courage to change countries and start operating in a completely foreign environment. And once upon a time, I too, veered through roads daringly, before I got used to the traffic laws in America. While I feared for my life in the Uber that day, I also saw this intrepid girl with unquestioning faith, and somehow, I was alright.

Printed in the United States
by Baker & Taylor Publisher Services